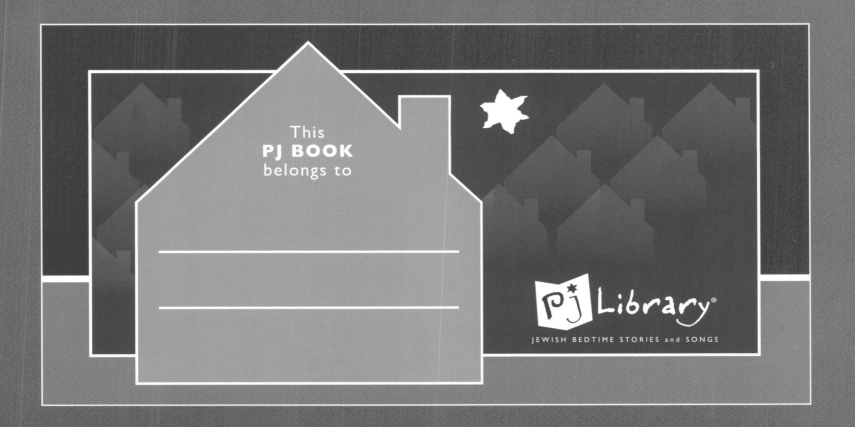

This
PJ BOOK
belongs to

_____

_____

PJ Library®

JEWISH BEDTIME STORIES and SONGS

Matzah Belowstairs

For Amira, Jasper, and Matthew, the new generation at the seder table. —S.L.M

To my dad, thank you for everything —M.E.

KAR-BEN PUBLISHING, INC.
A division of Lerner Publishing Group, Inc.
241 First Avenue North
Minneapolis, MN 55401 USA
1-800-4-KARBEN
Website address: www.karben.com

Main body text set in Beret LT Std Regular 15/19.
Tyepface proved by Linotype AG.

Library of Congress Cataloging-in-Publication Data

Names: Meyer, Susan Lynn, 1960- author. | Engell, Mette, illustrator.
Title: Matzah belowstairs / by Susan Lynn Meyer ; illustrated by Mette Engell.
Description: Minneapolis : Kar-Ben Publishing, [2019] | Series: Passover |
    Summary: A family of mice has no matzah for their Passover seder until
    Miriam, whose job is to forage, gets some unexpected help from the family
    that lives abovestairs. Includes facts about Passover.
Identifiers: LCCN 2018007309 (print) | LCCN 2018014498
    (ebook) | ISBN 9781541542136 (eb pdf) | ISBN 9781541521681 (lb : alk. paper) |
    ISBN 9781541521698 (pb : alk. paper)
Subjects: | CYAC: Mice—Fiction. | Matzos—Fiction. | Passover—Fiction. |
    Seder—Fiction. | Judaism—Customs and practices—Fiction.
Classification: LCC PZ7.M571751 (ebook) | LCC PZ7.M571751 Md 2019 (print) |
    DDC [E]—dc23

LC record available at https://lccn.loc.gov/2018007309

PJ Library Edition ISBN 978-1-5415-6427-5

Manufactured in China
1-46510-47546-9/5/2018

031926.4K1/B1352/A4

Matzah Belowstairs

Susan Lynn Meyer

illustrated by **Mette Engell**

KAR-BEN
PUBLISHING

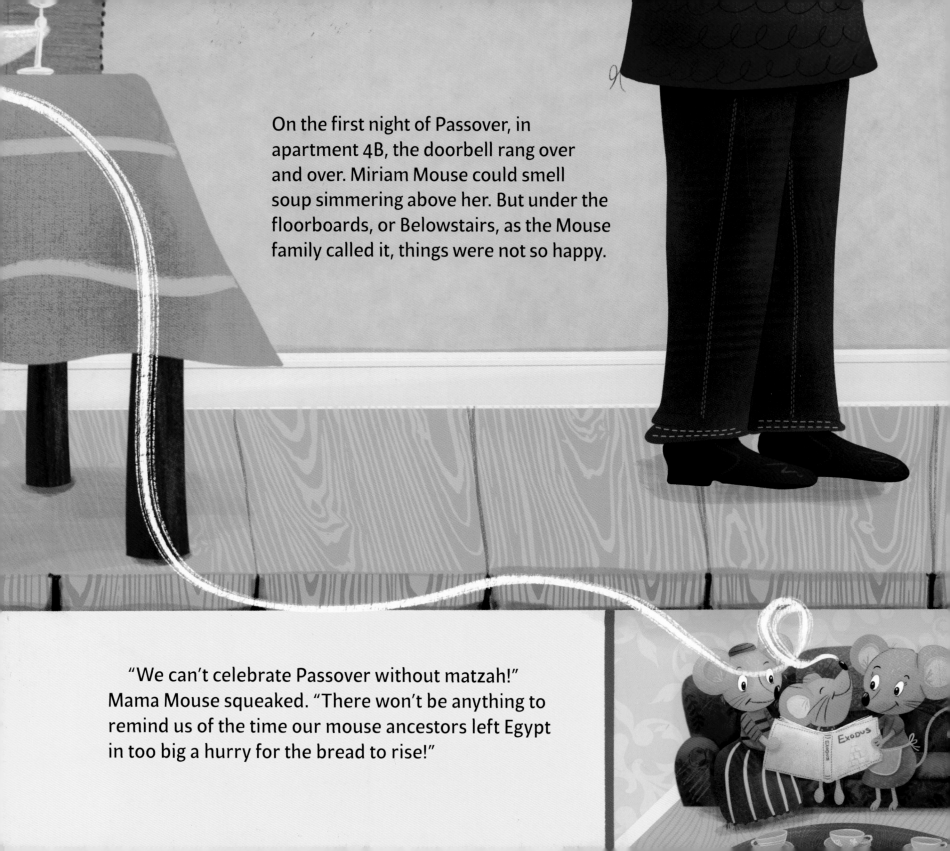

On the first night of Passover, in apartment 4B, the doorbell rang over and over. Miriam Mouse could smell soup simmering above her. But under the floorboards, or Belowstairs, as the Mouse family called it, things were not so happy.

"We can't celebrate Passover without matzah!" Mama Mouse squeaked. "There won't be anything to remind us of the time our mouse ancestors left Egypt in too big a hurry for the bread to rise!"

Miriam's whiskers drooped. She loved the crunchy, flat matzah they ate on the holiday. Foraging was her job. But she hadn't found any matzah for her family.

"It isn't your fault, Miriam," Grandpa Mouse said. "The Winklers usually leave lots of food around. It's just too bad they put the matzah in that new tin this year. Nobody could chew through that."

Miriam slipped away and climbed to her favorite spot behind Eli's chair. Eli often dropped food. Maybe he had dropped some matzah? But there wasn't a single matzah crumb on the floor.

The Passover seder Abovestairs was ready to begin. Eli's mother broke a piece of matzah and wrapped the afikomen in an embroidered napkin. "Dad will hide it and you can look for it at the end of the seder, Eli."

Someone always hid the afikomen as part of the Mouse seder, too, and searching for it with her cousins was Miriam's favorite part of Passover.

But without matzah, there would be no seder for the Mouse family.

As Miriam watched, Eli's dad slipped
the afikomen off the table.

Miriam darted behind the bookcase.

She heard footsteps, and suddenly a hand slid the afikomen under the bookcase.

Miriam's tail quivered with excitement. A huge piece of matzah was right in front of her.

The feet walked away, and Miriam heard Eli's family finishing the Passover meal.

"We need the afikomen to finish the seder," said Eli's dad. "Can you find it, Eli?"

As Miriam pushed and shoved, trying to squeeze the matzah into the mouse hole, she heard Eli running around the apartment, searching for the afikomen.

A face appeared on the other side of the bookcase. Eli looked at Miriam. Miriam looked at Eli.

"Hello, Mouse!" whispered Eli. "Do you want the afikomen?"

It was Miriam's big chance. But Eli needed the afikomen too. Without it, his family wouldn't be able to finish their seder.

Miriam thought for a moment. Then she hopped on the afikomen and snapped it in half.

Eli reached for a piece. "You keep the napkin," he whispered. "To help pull it."

"Thanks," squeaked Miriam. Eli winked and disappeared back into the dining room.

When Miriam appeared Belowstairs with the enormous piece of matzah, Grandpa Mouse chuckled in delight. "Enough for the whole week of Passover! Well done, Miriam!"

From Abovestairs came voices.
"Here's the afikomen!" Eli said.
"Where's the rest of it?" asked Eli's dad.

"And where's the napkin I embroidered?"
asked Eli's grandmother.
Eli shrugged. "Not there."

From Abovestairs, Miriam heard laughter, munching sounds and singing. "Hurry and set the table, Miriam," said Mama Mouse. "It's almost time for our seder to begin!"

Soon all the Mouse relatives had arrived. Miriam brought
her cousins into her room.
"Ooh!" squeaked Chloe.
"Are we going to play camp out?" squealed Amira.

"Sort of," said Miriam dreamily. "After dinner, we're going to pretend to be Israelite mice, escaping from Egypt and camping in the desert. Then I have a thank-you present to deliver!"

The Story of Passover

The first Passover happened long ago in the far-away country of Egypt. A mean and powerful king, called Pharaoh, ruled Egypt. Worried that the Jewish people would one day fight against him, Pharaoh decided that these people must become his slaves. As slaves, the Jewish people worked very hard. Every day, from morning until night, they hammered, dug, and carried heavy bricks. They built palaces and cities and worked without rest. The Jewish people hated being slaves. They cried and asked God for help. God chose a man named Moses to lead the Jewish people. Moses went to Pharaoh and said, "God is not happy with the way you treat the Jewish people. He wants you to let the Jewish people leave Egypt and go into the desert, where they will be free." But Pharaoh stamped his foot and shouted, "No, I will never let the Jewish people go!" Moses warned, "If you do not listen to God, many terrible things, called plagues, will come to your land." But Pharaoh would not listen, and so the plagues arrived. First, the water turned to blood. Next, frogs and, later, wild animals ran in and out of homes. Balls of hail fell from the sky and bugs, called locusts, ate all of the Egyptians' food.

Each time a new plague began, Pharaoh would cry, "Moses, I'll let the Jewish people go. Just stop this horrible plague!" Yet no sooner would God take away the plague than Pharaoh would shout: "No, I've changed my mind. The Jews must stay!" So God sent more plagues. Finally, as the tenth plague arrived, Pharaoh ordered the Jews to leave Egypt.

Fearful that Pharaoh might again change his mind, the Jewish people packed quickly. They had no time to prepare food and no time to allow their dough to rise into puffy bread. They had only enough time to make a flat, cracker–like bread called matzah. They hastily tied the matzah to their backs and ran from their homes.

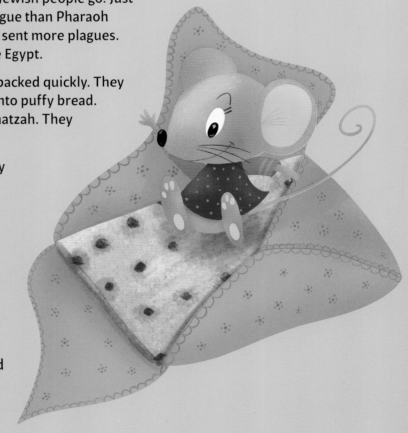

The people had not travelled far before Pharaoh commanded his army to chase after them and bring them back to Egypt. The Jews dashed forward, but stopped when they reached a large sea. The sea was too big to swim across. Frightened that Pharaoh's men would soon reach them, the people prayed to God, and a miracle occurred. The sea opened up. Two walls of water stood in front of them and a dry, sandy path stretched between the walls. The Jews ran across. Just as they reached the other side, the walls of water fell and the path disappeared. The sea now separated the Jews from the land of Egypt. They were free!

Each year at Passover, we eat special foods, sing songs, tell stories, and participate in a seder—a special meal designed to help us remember this miraculous journey from slavery to freedom.